WICKED CANDY

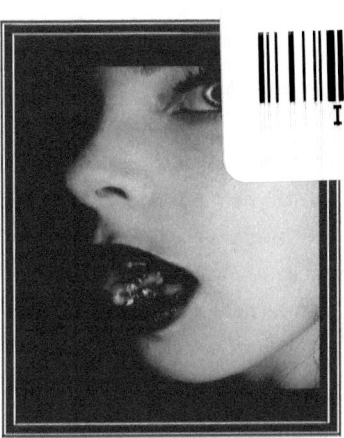

By **Alex S. Johnson**

And brought to you

From the friendly sociopaths at

Welcome To MorbidbookS. Where Everything Bleeds.

WICKED CANDY is published in the US and A by
MorbidbookS and the Grace of God.

Morbidbooks Is A Grotesque Bizarro Ballet Where The Most Profane Things Occur. An Impious And Perverse Dwelling Of Dark Revulsion. A Cozy Cottage Where Torture Porn And Brutal Bible Tales Are Devised. A Quiet Place To Relax And Spin Tales Of Depravity And Wickedness. A Halfway House For The Disturbed Where Rules No Longer Apply. A Safe Haven For Deviant Serial Killers To Hatch Their Wretched Schemes. Bring Your Pets. The Tasty Ones Are Always Welcome.

https://www.morbidbooks.wordpress.com

TABLE OF CONTENTS,

•   *"Vampussy" appeared previously in two parts in The Surreal Grotesque in slightly different form. All other stories are original to this collection.*

-0- PREFACE

NOW, NORMALLY WHEN I PREFACE SOMETHING, it
is not a good thing. It usually entails me holding my
hands up defensively and trying to explain a situation
before someone walks in on one hell of a mess that I
am somehow responsible for. Many times have I said
to my wife, "Now, let me preface this by saying…" to
try and cushion a blow of some type. That is not the
case here. But, in a way, that is totally the case here. So
when I was asked to preface Wicked Candy for Alex S.
Johnson, the first thing I did was look up the
definition of the word preface. A preface is usually an
opportunity for an author to explain or apologize for
the work that lurks and pulls on the chains behind his
words. Apologize? Fuck that. If you have never read
the work of Alex S. Johnson, then I will apologize for
the time it took you to discover this talented and
bizarre wordsmith. Alex lives in his own world, plays
by his own rules and mixes genres like a demented
chemist. The tales collected here would fail miserably
in lesser hands. But with Alex, you get stories that
could have come from a child-bearing orgy between
Hunter S. Thompson, Mel Brooks and Stephen King

while Nietzsche and Freud looked on and whacked off to the proceedings. Okay, so I will apologize for that bit of imagery. No one deserves that in their heads. When I make a reader laugh, it is as satisfying to me as making them gasp. Alex can pull either from you many times in a single paragraph. He boldly commits to the lunacy, and it pays off. One thing I can't tell you about Alex is what goes on in that brilliant but tortured and I am sure brightly-colored mind of his. Because it is a place I would never explore on my own. That is one rainbow I have no desire to chase. I trust Alex to responsibly deliver his madness to the paper. I do not need to see the machine behind it. The man is a mad and genre-defying genius. If you like to laugh, shiver, gag and you can appreciate the calculated and dark artistry of a man who is clearly insane in all of the right ways; you should tangle with this collection. After all, what tastes better than candy? Wicked candy, baby.

–Terry M. West
1–20–14

-1- THE FINAL FINAL GIRL

SALLY BAINBRIDGE WAS SICK of running. She could still hear them behind her, steady and tireless as robots—the guy with the ski mask and the six-inch serrated blade, the dude with the chainsaw and the mask of human skin, the man who wore a Donald Duck mask and brandished a squeaky toy. They'd been chasing her for hours through the forest and in the process she'd lost most of her clothes and was reduced to a frilly bra and thong panties, both shredded and filthy. Her hair was a beyond bedhead disaster, her cheeks were streaked with the dried trails of her tears, cold sweat was dripping down her ass-crack one icy drop at a time, and her kootchie smelled like rancid meat. Makeup? Forget about it—completely ruined. The only thing she could still boast about was her great muscle tone.

Her pursuers, on the other hand, were doing just fine. While her skin was cut and nicked and punctured from thorns and brambles and branches, they were barely scratched. While she was breathing heavily, had a stitch in her side, cramps in her legs and was almost overwhelmed with fatigue, they forged on powerfully to the accompaniment of cool theme music and/or sound effects. Sally found these conditions simply wrong and definitely unfair. It was time for a game change.

She stopped in her tracks and put her head down, hands on her thighs, until she had caught her breath. Then she turned around, squared her shoulders, placed her hands on her hips and faced her would-be attackers.

"This," she said, "is fucking ridiculous. We need to talk."

Ski Mask halted. He was wearing a heavy plaid shirt, black work pants and thick-soled boots. He passed his blade from one hand to another and closely examined the edge. Chainsaw Dude halted too, a few seconds later. He had on a brown flannel shirt, jeans and sneakers. He trailed his fingers across the two-stroke engine and then, with a sigh, lowered the saw. Donald

Duck mask, in a V-neck blue sweater, blue corduroys and Croc's, squeezed the squeaky toy.

"Now that I have your attention," she said, "well, most of it—Duck Boy, lose the toy, it's getting on my last nerve. My name is Sally Bainbridge. You all know me. I'm the final girl. The survivor. The one who returns for the sequels. The one who educates the other would-be victims and explains how the killers got to be so freaky."

Ski Mask ran a gloved hand over his blade. Chainsaw Dude fondled his weapon of choice. Duck Boy held up the squeaky toy to his ear, then squeezed it again. He made a gurgling, satisfied noise deep in his throat.

"Duck Boy here may be slightly challenged, but I don't think he's going to wreak much damage with the squeaky toy, other than *driving me fucking crazy*. So here's the deal. You guys clearly have some hang-ups. Big ones. My guess is it has something to do with your relationship with your mother. She fucked you up, so naturally you see all women as the enemy and want to fuck *them* up. Kind of a primitive logic, but hey—it gets you up in the morning. So we're going to do a little therapy session. Make a few emotional connections. Tie up some loose ends. First up, you with the ski mask. Tell me about Mommy, grisly details and all. And don't give me that catatonic mutism bullshit. We're going to settle this thing now."

"My mother…oh man. You really want to hear this? She dressed me up in girlie clothes and said she would cut off my—my wanger if I so much as thought about sex. Then she locked me in a closet with all these pictures of Jesus and wouldn't let me out until Jesus forgave me. Which never happened, so…I spent a lot of time in that closet. After that, it's pretty much of a blur. I set a lot of fires. Wet the bed. Then I started in with the animal torture. Gerbils, mostly. Wasn't so much torture as….let's just say most of them died from suffocation. They were so cute, I couldn't bring myself to, you know, rip them or anything, so I put them, uh, back there. Up my ass. After awhile they stopped struggling and then I had to dig out their little bodies and dispose of them. It got really messy. But I didn't want to do it. I was compelled. My mom's voice was in my head 24/7. I started having these feelings of rage, you know, just out-of-control hatred at anything female. The gerbils made me feel better. More complete, I guess.

"I began to stalk girls. I would follow them home and…watch them. Sometimes they left the blinds open and I saw them undress. That made me feel…funny. I was aroused but I wanted to hurt them too, like, stuff their panties down their throat and blind them with scissors. I'd hide in a tree and whack off and cut myself and used my own blood as lube. Then one time…"

Sally held up a hand. "Good start. Liking the honesty. Okay, let's hear from Chainsaw Dude."

"Yeah, uh, hey. My story is pretty much the same as Ski Mask here, only much, much more intense. My mom didn't just threaten to cut off my ding-a-ling, she lopped it off with a Ginzu knife and fed it to our Yorkshire Terrier, Fluffy. My rage was like, way advanced. I skipped right past the serial triad—bed-wetting, setting fires and torturing animals are cool and everything, don't know about gerbils, but whatever flicks your Bic—and started collecting trophies when I was 10. By the time I was 15 our back yard was a fucking cemetery, girls stacked up on top of each other. Can't remember when I started slicing their faces and tits off and wearing them myself, but it was pretty early in the game. Not only that, I..."

"Good, okay, we'll get back to you in a moment," said Sally. "So basically, all of you have deep-seated sexual neuroses stemming back to years of abuse and mistreatment. Except for Duck Boy here, who seems to have stumbled in from the wrong genre. *Not* one of us."

Ski Mask grunted. "Oh hells yeah," said Chainsaw Dude. "'Gooble gobble, we accept her.' Fucking *love* that movie."

"Me too. But back to my point. Hey, believe me, I get it. I have depression, anxiety, post-traumatic stress disorder, body dysmorphic disorder, irritable bowel syndrome, hyper-vigilance, trouble sleeping, hives, shingles, migraine headaches and jumpy bladder, among other symptoms. I can't keep a job for more than a week at a time. My social skills are totally shot. I haven't had a date in five years. Wanna know why? Anybody? Okay, I'll tell you. Because all my dates end up getting hacked to death by guys like you!

"You're not alone in feeling isolated and frustrated and lonely and horny and ready to wax a chump. I get it! But do you see me running around with a spear gun or a hacksaw? Have I ever eviscerated someone just so I could run my hands through their steaming guts, in lieu of, I don't know, getting off? Don't think so. And it's not like I haven't thought about it. In fact, these days almost all I think about is screaming bloody homicide. Gee, I wonder why.

"So here is what's up. I'm the Final Girl. Which means you don't get to kill me. Ever. Sure, you can scare me, chase me, pop up from under my bed and rush out of the closet or *what*-ever, but the rules of the genre dictate no killing the Final Girl. Okay, a little stabbing action here, hell, some grab-ass, kidnapping, Kinbaku, golden showers, menophilia. Suck my tampons all you want—more where that came from. But you can't kill me. Which sucks, I know, because it messes with the total body count. Hey, I didn't make the rules, so stop looking at me with those puppy dog eyes. I'm talking to you, Duck Boy! What's that you've got in your pocket? Come on, hand over the squeaky toy."

"No. Mine."

"I just want to see it. You've had it for a long time. Don't you want to share?"

"Um, er…okay." Hesitantly, he placed the toy in her outstretched palm.

"Very good Duck Boy. Now watch carefully." Sally hurled the toy as far as she could into the forest. There was a slight sploshing sound, then silence.

Duck Boy screamed, a loud, blood-curdling howl of anguish. Ski Mask covered his ears. Chainsaw Dude looked longingly at his chainsaw. "Hey," he said finally. "Do you think I might…"

"Oh, what the hell," said Sally. "Go for it."

Chainsaw Dude revved up the saw and beheaded Duck Boy with a few capable swipes. His head fell to the ground and his body followed a few minutes later once it realized what had happened to the head. "Thanks," said Chainsaw Dude. "I just had to get that out of my system.

"No worries," said Sally. "And thank you too, actually. Okay, so anyway—and please put the saw back on the ground, that thing makes me nervous—as I was saying, I'm just your average hot, busty 19-year-old girl. I'm not a heroine by any stretch of the imagination. Wasn't looking to get into the horror gig, that's for sure. A little stripping to pay my way through college, I don't know, condo in Boca, millionaire boyfriend to buy me lots of bling, that kind of thing. But oh no. You guys"—she plucked a rock from the ground and began to hammer Duck Boy's head into a sloppy cipher—"you guys had different plans for me. Like, spending half my time fending off chainsaws and knives when I'm not running for my life. I'm not complaining so much about that part, because you can see the results. Oh, stop drooling, you pervs. Nice little hardbody, huh? Sweet six pack? Well guess what—you're not getting *any* of this! Yes, Chainsaw Dude, you had a question?"

"Uh, yeah. What's Kinbaku?"

"Japanese rope bondage. Literally, 'the beauty of tight binding.' Not your style—takes too much patience and self-control. Anyway, I want you to leave me alone. All of you. That means no chasing, no attacks, no mutilation and absolutely no, under any conditions, killing me. Let's put it this way—if you kill me, you are banned from horror. Forever. Excommunicated. Banished. Shunned. Think about it. You'll have to get a whole new career. Shave every day. Bathe. Clip your nails. Get yourselves some professional clothes. And if you even think about scaring somebody, much less stuffing a corpse with tasty treats and beating it like a piñata, you go straight to Horror Jail, which is just like Disneyland, but much more smarmy. *Everybody* in Horror Jail wears the happy face and *The Sound of Music* is on auto-play. Not the Julie Andrews version. The other one. The wardens dress like chipmunks and…" She shuddered. "And you don't want that. Or do you?"

"All right, I've got a question," said Ski Mask.

"Go for it."

"You make some really good points. I mean, I never really thought about any of that stuff before. You get caught up in it, the chasing and the strangling and stabbing and eye-gouging, pretty soon you lose perspective. I can't speak for Chainsaw Dude here, but I think you deserve to be left alone. Hell, we can't kill you, so going after you is a pointless waste of time and energy. Only thing though is, well, I'm a serial killer. Always have been, always will be. It's what I do. So I guess what I'm asking is…"

"Let's put it this way," said Sally. "I don't give a fuck what you guys do for fun. Waste a bitch. Waste a whole lot of bitches. Take as many trophies as you need to. Keep the bodies around for company. Turn them into jerky, make lampshades out of their pussies, *I don't care*. I just want my life back. I wasn't cut out for this job. Didn't ask for it, didn't want it, don't need it. I'm just not Final Girl material. I just want to go home, take a long, hot shower, put on something decent that isn't crusted with blood and man gravy, maybe smoke a bowl, watch some stupid TV. All right? Are we all on the same page here?"

"Oh, cool," said Ski Mask. "Chainsaw Dude, are you good with that?"

Chainsaw Dude shrugged. "Yeah, whatever." They were silent for a moment. Then, "seriously, you have a thing for gerbils?"

Ski Mask pulled off the mask and ran his fingers through long, unkempt flaxen hair. His eyes were pale blue. A long, ragged scar cut across his face from just below his left eye to where his beard began. "Yeah, man," he said. So what?"

"That's a little gay. But like I said, whatever floats your boat."

"It has nothing to do with sexual preference. And for the record, I am 100% hetero. Unlike some people, I've actually been with girls. Or I could. At least I have the equipment for it."

"Hey, that is hitting way below the belt."

"So to speak."

"Permission to chump-wax?" asked Ski Mask.

"Permission very much granted," said
Sally.

Ski Mask lunged at Chainsaw Dude with
the blade. He swiftly cut his throat and stabbed
him in the heart. Gushing blood, Chainsaw Dude
staggered in a circle and then collapsed on his
face.

The atmosphere went from bleak and gray
to soft and diffuse. A golden ray of light peeked
through the trees and began to spread. Music
swelled from an unknown source.

There was an awkward silence. "So, uh,
what do we do now?"

"I guess we just hang out for a while," said
Sally. "Until…you know."

Three minutes later, Chainsaw Dude's
body had vanished.

"What happened, man?" asked Ski Mask.
"Animals drag him off or something?"

"You wish," said Sally, watching with
detached amusement as Chainsaw Dude suddenly
sprang up from behind Ski Mask, saw roaring.
The saw came down and neatly bisected Ski
Mask. The two pieces fell apart in a shower of

pus, blood, lymph and bile. Ski Mask's intestines pooled out and lay on the ground in a steaming pile. Chainsaw Dude lowered the saw and glared meaningfully at Sally. She shook her head. Then he too fell down and lay, finally, still.

"Well, this has been fun, but I gotta go," said Sally.

She heard noises in the forest. Branches cracked. Twigs snapped. A pair of wrinkled hands shot out, black with rot.

"Great, a zombie." Sally picked up the chainsaw and waited.

The zombie emerged from the trees. Half his face was missing. One eye drooled out on its stalk while the other eye socket swarmed with maggots. A cloud of flies buzzed around him. His overalls were falling off what was left of his shoulders.

Sally lifted the chainsaw. The heft of it, its solid weight, felt good in her hands. She caressed the cutting chain and carefully picked off the meat still clinging to it. A surge of giddy glee shot through her body as she raised the chainsaw above her head and brought it down on the zombie. Bits and shreds of grey flesh showered the air. She took her time with the decapitation, enjoying herself.

Finally, she stopped. A pool of blood was spreading across the ground from the mound of body parts. Eyeballs gleamed from a soup of guts, bones and bodily fluids.

"Gooble gobble, we accept her," said Sally softly under her breath. "One of us. One of us."

Maybe, just maybe, she did belong in the genre after all. Just not as the Final Girl.

END.

-2- VAMPUSSY

"ARE YOU SURE YOU'RE GOING TO BE OKAY?"

Jill Slutkin slumped against the wall, breathing heavily. Her best friend, Lydia X. Macabre, felt helpless. Slutkin had been on a downward spiral for several days now, binge drinking and gobbling party drugs like candy. Only last night, Lydia had found Jill curled up in a ball on the doormat in front of her apartment, her teeth chattering, her eyes unfocused, a thin thread of semen running down her torn fishnets. Her eyebrows and chin were coated with spunk and she smelled like a rotting fish.

Now, again, Jill was sweating, groaning and heaving. "Sure, I'm fine," she said, her voice barely audible. "I just need to do some more blow. Where's my fucking purse?"

"You sold it for blow," said Lydia. "Don't you remember anything? You were shouting 'Bling for Blow' over and over, like some degenerate mantra. The bartender had you 86'd. It was an ugly scene."

"I guess I'm just a nasty old slut," slurred Jill.

"No you're not," said Lydia, crouching beside her friend. "Look at me," she said, holding Jill's face in her hands. "I mean, really look at me."

"I—I can't," sobbed Jill. "My eyes are all crazy. I just see this big-ass blur. Is that you, or just Post-Impressionism? Do you still love me? Does anybody love me? How could you love a broken-down tramp who gets fucked up every night and fucked silly by anything with a dick?"

"Of course I love you," said Lydia. "I've been there, remember?"

"I can't remember shit," said Jill.

"But you will, once you get some help. Don't beat yourself up now. None of this is your fault."

"It's not?" said Jill. "Hey, you're kind of hot for a girl blur."

"I'm not going to leave you in this alley, that's for sure," said Lydia. "Wait, look"—she fished in her purse for her cell phone—"I'm going to call you a cab. We're gonna wait together until he gets here, and then you're going to go straight home and right to bed. We'll talk about it tomorrow."

"You're the bes' fren ever," said Jill, vomiting copiously on Lydia's shoes.

Ten minutes later, Lydia's cell buzzed. "Hello?" It was the cab company, something about heavy traffic uptown and the driver being on his way.

"Shit, okay, listen Jill, the cab is coming. I need you to just wait here for it. Don't try to move." She pulled a crumpled-up plastic garbage bag out of her purse. "Try to void your stomach as much as you can before you get into the cab, then if you still need to, you can use this. I just remembered, Von and I are supposed to have dinner at his place. I'd give you a ride, but his apartment is in midtown, going the opposite way."

"Don't worry," said Jill. "I'll be fine."

Five minutes after Lydia left, Jill heard a strange rustling noise coming from the end of the alley, where it led off from Buñuel Boulevard. A noise like wings.

Bat's wings.

She had no time to react, defend herself or even register what was happening before the creature was upon her, lap-dancing on her face. She felt two sets of razor-sharp teeth clamp down on her cheeks, talons gripping her temples. Inhaled the reek of bloody, unwashed pussy. Then a thick, flesh pole rammed itself down her throat.

She felt the vomit rising around the invasive organ, choking her as it forced its way deeper, and deeper. There was a hot, stinging sensation in her throat, then gurgling and slurping noises, followed at length by a thick, sour discharge. Her vision swam, and she blacked out.

●●●

The Making of a Monster (Two Weeks Earlier)

Dr. Herman Groinslab Patted the lead-lined glass box. "What we have here," he said, "is a triumph of genetic retrofitting. The ordinary human vagina, enhanced by its union with the vampire bat."

"And it's got dentata," observed Dr. Gimpel Slappy, Groinslab's hapless assistant.

"Of course it has teeth," fumed Groinslab. "And an enlarged clitoris that serves for interpenetration between the Vampussy. The end of the clitoris features a spike for piercing once the creature has a firm hold of the victim, and a hollow feeding tube at the bottom. These creatures are functionally bisexual, by which I mean that any two Vampussy can reproduce."

The beast slammed against the glass, leaving tooth marks and a streak of drool. "Oh hush, little one," said Groinslab affectionately. "She's feisty today. She's telling me not to forget the Coco Puffs."

"I thought they were strictly…carnivorous," said Slappy.

"Oh no, they're simply crazy for Coco Puffs," said Groinslab. "Haven't you heard a word I've been saying? Vampirism is merely an atavistic function of their DNA. I'm retraining them on sugary breakfast cereals. At first they become extremely agitated, then they go to sleep. But at the apex of their agitation, they mate, and when they do, we'll see a phenomenon hitherto unknown to science."

Dr. Slappy suddenly realized why his cereal supply was low. "You bastard," he said. "You uncouth, undignified bastard."

"I'd watch your tongue if I were you," said Groinslab imperiously. "And I mean that more literally than you think."

"Didn't mean any disrespect, Doctor," said Slappy.

But he did mean disrespect—and far worse. One day he would wreak a terrible vengeance on Groinslab, whose autocratic style had relegated Slappy to a humble, subservient position far beneath his skills and talents. And to think that they had both attended Miskatonic U. medical school at the same time, Dr. Slappy's MCAT scores soaring above those of his so-called friend. But that was then. Slappy's proclivity for rodents had been his undoing. If only he'd been more discreet—alas, Groinslab caught him in the act of insertion, and ever since then had tyrannized over his erstwhile bedmate and confidante.

"You said they can mate," said Slappy. "Have you created a pair?"

"This is the prototype," said Groinslab proudly. "And yes, I've got a pair." He retrieved a silver whistle from the pocket of his lab coat and blew into it.

"I can't hear anything," said Slappy.

"That's because it's a high-frequency signal," said Groinslab. "Only *they* can hear it."

There was the sudden rustle of wings. Slappy looked up to see a dark, hairy shape perched on an exposed utility pipe ten feet above his head. Then a drop of viscous liquid landed on his forehead.

Groinslab laughed. "She likes you," he said. "That's good luck."

"If they have multiple, bimodal sex organs, why do you refer to them all as 'she?'"

"Good question," said Groinslab. "The answer is that it's a purely arbitrary choice."

But it wasn't. They were all 'she' because of Her—cult icon Nico. Ibiza, the bicycle accident, the spontaneous ejection of Nico's pussy and its retrieval by lurking Warhol fetishists as the remainder of Nico's body was driven to hospital after hospital by a Samaritan taxi driver. The packing of Nico's pussy in dry ice, its preservation, super-sizing and plumping and, finally, the cloning experiments that ultimately resulted in the creatures that Groinslab had brought to life.

"Okay," said Slappy, attempting to wipe off the liquid with a handkerchief. "Still, I have so many questions. Yes, it's impressive that you've compiled, or composed, or invented these things. But why?"

"Why?" asked Groinslab. "Why ask why? Just look at them go!"

The other Vampussy had inserted its elongated clitoris into the hole in the glass box reserved for just such a function. For a moment the two creatures seemed to merge together in a gyrating fusion of dark hair, eyes and teeth. The sounds of their union were felt rather than heard—a kind of curdling of the air around them.

Slappy felt vaguely ill. "How long does this last?" he asked Groinslab. "I think I'm gonna hurl."

"This is the first time I've seen them in action," said Groinslab. "A beautiful sight, is it not? What was it that John Keats said…in 'Lamia'….or was it 'Labia?'"

Slappy peered at the rutting hybrids from between his fingers. "I'll admit that it's unusual, I don't know about beautiful. Although I suppose any natural phenomenon has its beautiful side."

"But don't you see," said Groinslab. "Don't you get it? It's the very unnatural quality of this pairing, the Satanic wrongness of it, that makes it so—sublime. Nature would never intend such a thing. This is the end, my friend, the end of laughter and soft lies."

"But I thought the laughter and soft lies would go on forever," said Slappy, pouting.

"Don't be a little bitch," said Groinslab. "You know what I mean."

The Vampussies had blurred into a flickering, fluctuating mass. "Once sexual ahem frenzy has been reached via a vigorous feeding, the clitori interpenetrate and discharge their DNA solution into one another. At this point, both Vampussy become 'charged,' as we say. However, I did not anticipate this part."

Groinslab groaned.

"What's happening?"

"I hope it's not what I think it is," said Groinslab. "Some of the sims showed this as a possibility, but a slim one."

The lab's atmosphere seemed to warp around them, sight reduced to a pulsating ball where the Vampussies interchanged attributes. Growing into one, then splitting off into thousands of tiny winged vajayjays that sparkled and winked out like Stephanie Meyers' career trajectory.

There was a loud explosion. A violet mist filled the air, gathering around the glass box. At the coital nexus, a corkscrew of ash-like particles drilled into an aperture that opened into the very fabric of spacetime. For a very brief moment, both doctors were transformed into hamsters with enormous, conical cocks on their foreheads.

The particle stream pulled the Vampussy ball into the vortex, and the aperture closed like a satisfied mouth. Leaving a jagged hole in the glass, curled and melted at the edges and still dripping.

Slappy had a nanosecond to ponder the consequences of life as a cock-headed space hamster before order was restored.

"What in the name of fuck was that all about?" gasped Slappy. "What happened? Where did they go?"

"Nowhere," said Groinslab. Then, on second thought, "everywhere. It's complicated. Quantum indeterminacy, the Heisenberg principle. Do you remember what you were thinking about when they started to…spawn?"

Slappy suppressed his actual memory, a thick, heady rage at the violation of his cereal horde. He then suppressed the subsequent memory, a tumescent, bulging lust for rodents.

"You were thinking about hamsters," said Groinslab. It was not a question, just an assertion of fact.

Slappy bowed his head, shamefaced. "I'm afraid you're right."

Groinslab put his arm around Slappy's shoulders. "You know, it could have been worse, much worse. My theory at this point is that your hamster lust somehow affected their mating. These creatures have a kind of allergy to rodents, I'm not sure why. Thus creating a warp in timespace and the implosion that we just saw. The Vampussy could be anywhere and nowhere. One thing's for sure, if they're loose in the general population, we're in for a shitstorm of freakiness."

●●●●

One Month Later

"Jill, Is That You?"

Lydia could barely believe her eyes. The last time she'd seen her friend, she'd been puking her guts up in an alley behind Club Jackoff, spunk crusted in her Betty Page bangs, her face sagging like a wet paper bag.

The woman she now saw, decorously sipping a double espresso, hands wandering idly through the glossy pages of *Bizarrina* magazine, was immaculate. She sported stylishly short blonde curls, her nails were manicured and bore the hippest new 'urban' polish, Toad Venom, which had barely hit the market. She wore a tastefully sexy pink blouse and a matching skirt with white silk stockings; as far as Lydia could tell, there were no rips, tears or unsightly gashes in her outfit.

She looked good. Better than good. Her face had lost ten years of wear, and her makeup was neatly applied.

"Yes, it's me darling," said Jill Slutkin, extending a hand encased in a white suede glove. "I'm sorry I didn't call. So many things have happened since that night."

"I was just going to grab a cup to go and then catch up on some editing from home," said Lydia. "Then I saw you. I was thinking wait, Jill? You look amazing."

"I feel amazing," said Jill. "That night changed everything."

Jill's powder blue eyes were clear and focused. "Sit down, join me for a second."

Lydia sat down across from her friend. "I feel really bad about just leaving you like that. So guilty."

"Please," said Jill. "It was the best thing you could have done for me."

"So you got home okay?"

"Well, the funny thing is that I don't remember how I got home. I was crouched down in that alley feeling like shit warmed over, and then—I was home. In my bed. I must have slept into the afternoon. It was like I just turned the page at the end of a chapter and suddenly everything was fresh and new. No hangover. Somehow I'd taken a bath and...washed the...stuff from my hair, got myself into my pink silk jammies, and bingo, I was well into the next day."

"So you don't remember anything about the cab, the ride home?"

"Nothing. But it's ok. I don't want to get all religious on you, but it was almost like a form of grace. I don't know how else to put it."

"Again, you look great. Really."

"Thank you. I think I just got sick and tired of being sick and tired, you know? All those nights I couldn't remember, coked up out of my mind, sausage in every hole, plus other stuff. It was enough already. I've turned that page. Joined a gym. I even got a little dog. A terrier puppy. My life's a lot more quiet now."

"So you don't miss it, the partying?"

"You saw how I was. I put through you a lot of shit. But I realized I had to start doing for myself, you know. I had to make the decision to turn it around, for me. For Jill. Not to say that my life's a cakewalk now, but I feel so much more at peace with myself."

"I'm really happy for you," said Lydia. "Maybe we could get together soon."

"Just give me a call. This is my new number"—she passed a scrap of paper across the table—"I had to get rid of the old one because so many scumbags had it. But the apartment's the same."

"I will, definitely. Well, I gotta run. Enjoy your day."

"Call me," said Jill.

●●●

Lydia Was Dreaming. She knew she was dreaming, and though the dream was dark, sinister and ominous, she couldn't shake herself awake. Something held her within it, like a cage around her chest.

She was sitting in a sunken, smoky bachelor den carpeted in ratty, torn puke-stained yellow-orange. Besides the acrid smell of cigar smoke, there was something else, a vaguely chemical odor. Burn holes riddled the carpet. Three rows of fold-out chairs held an audience of nine people, watching an amateurish 8 mm movie. The movie was silent except for the occasional burst of incidental sound effects.

In the movie, a tall, statuesque woman with henna-dyed hair and immaculate cheekbones was riding a bicycle alongside a young man. They were bantering and laughing soundlessly. The disparity between their ages suggested to Lydia either a cougarish predatory relationship or a familial one, or both. The two riders approached the camera but appeared not to be aware they were being filmed. Sunspots glared across the lens and the movie rattled in the projector.

Jump cut to the same two riders but filmed on a different stock. A brief flash of scratched black leader. Then back to the original film stock. Slow motion. As though acting in an early Expressionist movie, the woman dramatically clutched her chest and fell from her bicycle. Jump cut and extreme close-up of the young man's face as he expressed fear and terror and spoke soundlessly. There is a quick burst of distorted electric viola on the soundtrack. Another jump cut to what appears to be an outtake from a Fellini movie. The same woman is dancing on a table while nattily-dressed aristocrats swill champagne and ejaculate one another's fat cocks. A woman in clown makeup jumps up before the camera and gestures frantically towards something freshly written on the wall in dripping red letters.

Lydia hears the words "bicycle," "Ibiza" and "Nico icon" in her head. These words are not on the movie soundtrack. In the film, a taxi speeding by suddenly stops in a puff of dust, and the driver leaps out and runs to the side of the prone woman. With the help of the son, the taxi driver lifts the woman's limp body into the back of the taxi. There is a cut to a doctor examining a chart on a clipboard and shaking his head. Extreme close-up of some words scribbled at the bottom of the first page on the chart. Although they are in Spanish, Lydia's dreaming brain automatically translates them as "spontaneous ejection of subject's vagina, left gaping hole. Vagina not found." In another hand, someone has written the words "Tanit, heavenly goddess of war, related to Ishtar/Astarte." Cut to a man holding up a dripping vagina by henna-dyed pubic hair, as though it were a trophy. A scuttering and rustling like bat wings on the soundtrack.

Lydia awakes to find herself lashed to Jill's bed with leather restraints, a large ball-gag firmly secured in her mouth.

Jill sits in a chair next to the door. She is nude, pale, completely immobile. But for the faint rising of her chest, she could be dead. Her eyes are wide open, staring blankly.

Every square inch of the bedroom has been painted black. The lamps have black shades. The cabinets and chests of drawers are black. The bed Lydia lies in is fitted with black satin sheets.

The only light in the room comes from dripping clumps of goo splattering the walls, the ceiling, the carpet. The goo pulses, and as Lydia's eyes adjust she can see vein clusters within the clumps. She then sees that both Jill's body and her own are liberally slathered with the live, glowing goop.

She hears the thump and shake of something disengaging from the ceiling. As it flies into the shimmering halos of the goo clumps, it reveals itself as a creature—a nightmare hybrid, a vagina with bat wings.

Forgetting the ball-gag, she attempts to scream as the vag-bat flies closer, its leather wings gusting the thick, heady scent of unwashed pussy towards her face. The vaginal cavity opens, showing two vertical rows of razor-sharp teeth. A long, pink tongue descends from the clitoral hood, and a deep, sonorous voice emerges, with a thick German accent.

"So how do you like my new look? Not so much like a clown, *jawohl?*"

The voice is so familiar, but Lydia can't place it. A voice she has known since childhood. The way it pronounces the word "clown"—like KLAAAOOWN—sends shivers down her spine. But where had she heard it before? Some element was missing, the context.

"I see you are struggling to speak. I would very much like your impression of my appearance. Slave, release the prisoner's mouth!"

Robotically, Jill rises from the chair, bends over the bed and frees the ball-gag from Lydia's lips. Lydia began to recall the previous evening, the moment-by-moment transformation of her old friend into the zombie-like host of a ravening, winged pussy-creature. She remembers repeated penetrations of every hole she had—and some new ones—by the creature's outsized clitoris, the pussy-dick jammed down her throat, then hovering a few feet from her face, convulsing, clenching, exuding a pungent, tonic mist; a sharp, monstrous pain deep in her throat, the sensation of being fed upon, and then an explosion of hot jissom. The iridescent cum dripping down her forehead, her cheeks, her chin, so much more of it than she could swallow in one gulp, as the deep, Teutonic voice insisted that she be a good girl and take it all. Her face, tits, ass and pussy were still crusted with the stuff.

"What the fuck is going on?" Lydia rasped. "Who are you? What do you want? And what have you done with Jill?"

"I am the artist slash model slash chanteuse slash actress formerly known as Nico, now a hybridized, genetically-modified experiment, newly escaped from the lab. Is that not clearly obvious?"

"Oh, ok, now I get it," said Lydia. "That would explain why your voice sounds so familiar."

"Uff course eet's not as easy to make music as of old," said the Nico-pussybat, her accent thickening as the words squeezed from her labia.

"But before I die in bizarre bicycle accident on Spanish island of Ibiza, I learn to sing through diaphragm. So, simple transition to singing through poooooshy."

"Please tell me this is all a bad dream or some really good PCP or something," said Lydia. "I know I'm not crazy, but this is…it's wrong."

"Az my goot frend Jeem Morrison once told me, all life is staychess of tronsfoarmation— eez not typo, is phonetic approximation of Cherman haccent. Thees eez thee ent, my ooooonly frent, thee ent…"

"Let me get this straight," said Lydia. "You're a genetically-modified bat-pussy organism based on cult icon Nico, and you're using my friend's body as a host?"

"Basically, but eez more complicated. When Nico's poooooshy wass ejected spontaneously, eet was possessed by Carthaginian mother goddess Tanit, also known as Ishtar or Astarte. As Vampussy, I, Tanit, have returned to Earth to reclaim my domain. You may call me Vampusseria."

"I suppose that isn't any weirder than the rest of it," said Lydia. "So do you think maybe you could release me now?"

"I yoos your body as hincubaytor," said Vampusseria. "Like zo." The creature dove between Lydia's legs and drilled the clit-tongue deep into her womb. The pain was unbearable at first, but gradually, as Vampusseria buzzed and darted and supped like a hummingbird, it transformed into an eerie kind of pleasure.

Lydia was dimly aware of a deep, Germanic voice intoning the Velvet Underground classic "All Tomorrow's Parties" somewhere in the area of her cervix before she passed out, dreaming of crescent-headed fertility goddesses and endless tunnels inscribed with vagina-shaped symbols.

●●●

Johnny New One Was nursing a tall blue drink at the Pachyderm Bar in West Lulu when the doctor shambled in.

"I seen some things, man," said the doctor, quickly demolishing three margaritas in a row.

Always on the lookout for new screenplay material when not hustling his ass for blow, Johnny immediately took an interest in the man. "Thirsty work, eh?" he said as a conversation opener.

The man was wearing a lab coat streaked with blood, hair and something that closely resembled jissom, but with a different consistency and a slight glow to it. He wiped the sweat from his forehead with a cocktail napkin and answered Johnny, still staring into his margarita glass, "I'll have your answer in a second. First, total annihilation of consciousness. You wouldn't happen to have any elephant tranquilizer on you, by any chance?"

"No, man, that's heavy stuff. Hey, aren't you some kind of doctor? Why can't you write a script for yourself?"

"Grimpel Slappy, Miskatonic U. Medical School, class of '96. Pleased to meet you."

"Pleasure's mine, dude. So, uh, are you upset about something? Sometimes it helps to talk. Maybe you should slow down with those drinks."

"Talk? Sure. You seem like a friendly guy."

"What's all that stuff on your lab coat?"

"Oh, that? Mostly what it looks like. Listen buddy, my advice to you...is just walk away. I made my own bed, now I'm gonna lie down in it."

"It's all good," said Johnny. "I was just on my way to get my ass reamed for blow, but I've got about an hour till I gotta be at this guy's place. I'd really like to hear your story."

"You a reporter or something? 'Cause I tried to go to the press. They kicked me out of the office, the *Times*...some asshole in a bow tie. Say, who do you know w-wears a bow tie these days anyway?"

"No, I'm not a reporter. Sometimes I try my hand at writing screenplays, though."

"Doesn't matter. I jess need a fren, someone to lissen..." And Slappy proceeded to pour forth the saga of his woes, omitting no wet and shiny detail. At a few points Johnny was forced to slap his new friend forcefully to shake him off the subject of hamster farts and his yen for Coco Puffs, but over half an hour, the story emerged.

Johnny felt stunned, hammered, pole-axed and not in the good way. As the best-paid bun boy in Beverlywood and West Lulu combined, he had seen, heard and felt things to make the Marquis de Sade shit himself with disgust and loathing. But Dr. Slappy's story opened whole new vistas of depravity. And would make a great screenplay, once Johnny had done some research and expanded his knowledge of genetics, vampirism, quantum mechanics, wormholes in spacetime and the instability of certain vampire bat-pussy hybrids. All of which seemed to have some kind of esoteric relationship to a book titled the *Necronomicon*, by the mad Arab Abdul Alhazred and even suggest a way to defeat them. Or at least shut them out.

Apparently this was now a required textbook at Miskatonic U. The *Necronomicon* spoke of portals through which a race of transdimensional aliens, called The Old Ones or The Elder Gods, might slip into the mundane world for unknown purposes. Slappy had warned

Johnny of the consequences of investigating this book, but Johnny figured that it would help him understand the genesis of the Vampussy, and even suggest a way to defeat them, or shut them out.

Back in his cramped studio apartment in LaLaHood, Johnny Googled till his hands cramped. At first he retrieved a lot of garbage, websites that led him into virtual cul-de-sacs filled with pop-ups advertising something called "The Shwibly." But after solid effort, punctuated by frequent bathroom trips to douche his asshole of a loathsome combination of black tar heroin, spunk and fruit juice, he began to hit pay dirt. The seemingly random search words began to generate the same results, over and over, pointing to a club in West Lulu: Bela's Brew-Ha Ha.

That Friday afternoon, Johnny took Buñuel down to Jodorowsky and found the club, literally a hole in the wall. Stepping through the crack, he was accosted by a 6' 2" heavily muscled bald man, who seized him by the shoulders, head-butted him and flipped him over on his back.

"How you find this place?" asked the bouncer.

"I…uh…from your website? It has the street address right on it."

"Oh," said the bouncer. "Sorry. Internet. Sven is old school."

"You're Sven?"

"Yeah. Sven Lundquist. Sorry about the rough stuff. We get a lot of looky-loos here. You're not a looky-loo, are you?"

"I'm not sure what that even means," said Johnny. "Hey, could you give me a hand? I think you crushed my spinal column or something."

The bouncer extended a meaty hand. "Sure. Looky-loos are hipsters, you know, trash. Guys with ironic mustaches. Bald patches with the word 'hair' written on them."

Johnny unconsciously felt his own mustache. "Well yeah, I do have facial hair, but it's not meant to be ironic. Just a goatee. Say, what's the idea?"

"You come here for show?"

"Sure, I came here for a show. But now I think I need some elephant tranquilizers and a long sauna bath."

"You come with Sven, he fix you up."

After several elephant tranquilizers and a satisfying sauna, Sven gave Johnny a free back massage and readjusted his bones. "Show's on the house. You sit back and enjoy."

Oddly enough, Johnny's back felt better than before it had been recalibrated.

In front of a backdrop with a vaguely Dali-esque painting of rhinoceri coupling, some saggy-titted, overweight strippers performed a fairly conventional Three Stooges routine. A jittery clown played a Chopin piano etude as the waitresses, long, thin girls dressed as Gothic scarecrows, took drink orders. Johnny waved his hand in demurral, satisfied with the pachyderm tranks. Part of him wished he'd fled the bar as soon as the doctor showed up in the splattered lab coat with the frenzied story, but another part of him was hooked. He wanted to see how the whole narrative would unfold. Would it be happy feeding time at Pussy Palace, his veins coursing with novel drugs, or would it be the usual bukkake-dunking and dreary, wheezing evocation of a Weimar cabaret scene as he struggled to free himself from a man-sized Jello cube once again?

Johnny hated that whole Weimar Jello scene with a passion. He peered suspiciously at the dimly lit stage. Three spotlights made random Venn diagrams through purple gel, revealing a resinous stain on the floor. On closer inspection, the stain took on a Weimar Jello aura and Johnny closed his eyes shut, emphatically squeezing out *those particular memories.*

Then a new clown sat down at the piano and began to play a slow, doomy intro. Dry ice poured across the stage, and an oddly shaped shadow poured itself across the painting. Johnny wiped his eyes and saw what was projecting the shadow. And felt an icy sensation in his guts.

It was her—the creature from Slappy's narrative. Vampusseria.

"I am zoooo ferry eggsited to be here with you today," droned Vampusseria. "As some of you know, I haff bin mekking a few unannounced appearances at local clubs promoting my new owl-boom, which iss afailable in download form only. Eet iss called Neeco Poooshy. You all should hear it. Some uff my very best werk."

Vampusseria landed on a table, and took a few drags from a long ebony cigarette holder it held in its talons. Exhaling a cloud of blue smoke from its labia, the former cult icon turned pussybat tapped its claws, as though tuned in to her own personal radio station.

"I now sing medley of greatest heets," she said.

The club was starting to fill up now. Hipsters of every description sauntered in, some completely nude, others shrink-wrapped in cellophane. They exuded a palpable aura of decadence, exhaustion with everything, a world-weariness that went far beyond standard-issue ennui. Their skin writhed with complex tattoos featuring Mom, bison, lanced reptiles and several varieties of cheese-creatures. Johnny noted that a few of the hipsters even sported eyeball piercings and had the haunted, furtive look familiar to acolytes of socket sodomy.

The hipsters assumed elaborate worshipful attitudes before the stage, clustering together before their idol.

Nico pussybat spread her wings over them as they gathered in, yearning for just a taste of that splendid, salty, hypertrophied clitoris. They nipped at the end and clamped their teeth to its sides, jostling for a chance to suck it. The pussybat picked up a microphone.

"Thee sees the ent, my only frent, thee ent..."

As the lyrics issued from her lips, the hipsters began to writhe in ecstasy, performing spirited whip-dances in tribute to Gerard Malanga. A DAT backing tape played an accompaniment through hidden speakers— shrieking synthetic noises, like rubberized insects splattering against a windshield, stabbing riffs from an electric guitar, as the rhythm quickened. The melody became jangled, incoherent, matched by the frenzied movements of the hipsters.

"Lost in a Roman veelderness uff pain..."

They were tearing raw hunks from one another, lips foaming with blood. Johnny watched in shock and amazement as the hipsters ground against each other, as the Nicopussybat gyrated above them, feeding on them as they fed on one another. The stage was awash with a widening pool of blood and jissom, flecked with organ meats.

As the song arced to its climax, the Oedipal allegory of the killer in the ancient gallery, the worshippers looked whipped and buffeted by psychic winds, some half-skeletal now, slippery clusters of nerves sliding through new holes that opened up in chests and shoulders and legs, a process of erosion working its way through the dancing flesh. Johnny scanned the room for an exit, and saw a light coming from a door to the right of the stage.

But what if they spotted him? He had to take that chance. If he stayed, he'd be swallowed up in the ravening maw of the ritual. Ducking his head down and scurrying past the stage like an insect, Johnny didn't bother to check if they saw him or not. He finally breathed the cold outside air with a mixture of relief and lurking fear. He could still hear the music playing, the coda, winding down now as the song ended.

Now what was he going to do? He made his way through the parking lot and raced down the street, past shuttered storefronts and gas stations, trying to put some distance between himself and the mad scene he'd just witnessed.

Finally, he could run no longer. He slumped against a wall, breathing hard, sweat pouring down his face. When he heard the voice: "Meeester Johnny, you left beefor all ze fun!"

I am so fucked, thought Johnny.

•••

Von Hulking Swabbed Himself with a towel, laid it back on the workout bench and picked up the cell phone. It was Lydia's voice mail.

"Lydia, I've been trying to call you for days. What happened to you? Get back in touch."

He went back to doing reps with the free weights when something on the TV screen over his head caught his eye. They were interviewing some guy; Von couldn't hear what he was saying, but the closed captioned translation had something to do with a savage attack that had taken place the previous night, four blocks from Lydia's apartment.

With an ashen face, the man was talking some gibberish about fertility rituals, bicycles in Ibiza, a hybridized bat-creature and experiments sourced from a forbidden book that was at the same time available in many editions and easily acquired—even in the version used by students at Miskatonic University Medical School. The reporter repeated the information that 15 people, members of the local art community, had mysteriously disappeared, and that the man had purportedly witnessed some kind of awful celebration in which flesh had been torn and devoured. He himself had barely escaped with his life.

Von found the TV station's phone number on his iPhone and called. They didn't have any more information than the report had given, but Von told them he had a sinking feeling about his girlfriend, Lydia X. Macabre.

"She hangs with those guys, yeah, the art punks. That neighborhood is pretty sketchy. She tried to get me to see some shows there, but the one thing I saw, some dude was eating a dead cat and vomiting it back up. Not quite my scene, you know? No wait, don't hang up. She's disappeared. I haven't heard from her, and I called the antique store she works at part-time and she hasn't come in. I'm afraid something has happened to her. Something connected with all this weirdness."

The reporter took Von's information and asked him to stay in touch.

Later that night, Von Hulking drove by Lydia's apartment. He buzzed her door several times and banged on it, to no avail. The mail slot was crammed and letters spilled out from under the door.

He was now convinced that there was a connection between her disappearance and that of the hipsters. But what was the missing link? If only he could get in touch with the man who'd seen it all go down. Johnny New One.

Von scratched his bald head. That such a familiar name. But where had he heard it before? He suddenly recalled the context, and his face flushed with the memory. Ordinarily he didn't party, but there had been that one night, the specifics blurred but punctuated with imagery of hairy guys—'bears,' they had called themselves—and lots of nose candy. Von had been doing a heavy exercise regimen in preparation for the Mr. Pecs contest, and now that he'd taken home another trophy, he could afford to loosen up a little bit.

Johnny New One wasn't a bear, but he had buried himself in Von Hulking's mighty gluteal muscles, and the two had climaxed together not once, not twice, but three times in succession.

"And I'm not even gay," recalled Von Hulking. Still, he liked to think of himself as open-minded.

Von flicked through his saved phone numbers. Sure enough, there was a listing for a "Nu1." That had to be the guy.

"Yeah?" said a shaky voice on the other end.

"You don't know me, but my name is Von Hulking. We have to talk."

•••

A Week Later, Von Hulking was sitting in a lawn chair in his back yard when a miracle occurred: his stone angel shed tears of blood.

He and Johnny New One had spent the days in between talking, pooling information and planning. Lydia was still missing, the TV reporter had uncovered nothing new, and the two found themselves alone against a terrible menace, so strange and inscrutable they could barely discuss it between themselves. The terms "Nico Pussybat" and "spontaneous vaginal disembodiment" were not part of either's usual vocabulary.

"So, they're vampires, basically," said Von Hulking on the third day, sometime in the late afternoon. The two had been gobbling their way through their combined drug hoards and were fairly disconnected from consensual reality. "How do you get rid of vampires?"

"Dude, they're not just ordinary vampires. They're genetically modified creatures of total darkness. I've been doing some research, but I keep coming up against this stone wall. People are either afraid to talk about it, or you and I have made ourselves victims of a shared delusion. It's been known to happen."

"All I know is this," said Von Hulking. "We have to fight them. In the movies, that means a cross, holy water, garlic. Not necessarily in that order."

"It can't hurt," said Johnny.

Thus it was that Von had experienced the miracle of the blood-weeping angel and had summoned the closest thing he could find to a priest, Father Fritter, an old half-blind schizophrenic who once played the part of a priest on reality TV.

"I'm pretty sure it's a miracle," said Von Hulking. "Look at all that blood flowing. It reminds me of the Mister Pecs contest back in '08, when I got hold of some bad juice and my six-pack exploded. Let me tell you, I was not bulking out for quite awhile. My recovery was long and painful."

Father Fritter squinted at the statue. "I may just be an old half-blind schizophrenic who once played the role of a defrocked priest on reality TV, but I'm pretty sure that's not an angel, Von. That's a lawn gnome. And somebody spilled ketchup on it. Hideous. Aesthetically, I mean."

"It's a good thing for you I've got a strangulated hernia from working out or you'd be in for a world of pain, Father," said Von Hulking. "I hope you brought the rosary and the cross so we can get this blessing started."

"You're a fucking idiot," muttered Father Fritter.

"I hope you didn't mutter something that will earn your ass a world of pain," growled Von Hulking.

"I said, 'let's get on with it,'" said Father Fritter. He knelt before the lawn gnome and made the sign of the cross. "I hereby sanctify this bucket of water in the name of the most high. God, please charge this water with your wrath and vengeance so that my good friend Von here may wreak chaos and grim death upon the Vampussies. In the name of the big one, the little one and the misty one. Amen."

"Aren't you supposed to command it with the power of Christ?"

"That's an exorcism, you fool," said Father Fritter.

"Oh," said the bodybuilder. "Okay, you are dismissed."

"Where's the money?"

"It's a good thing I'm wearing a truss right now so my insides won't spill out, or I'd be wailing on your ass like Bob Marley. I thought you priests worked for the common good. Now you're asking for money?"

"Yeah well, like I said, I'm only a half-blind schizophrenic actor who once played the role of a defrocked priest on reality TV, so, some cash would be nice. Like maybe fifty bucks?"

"Look, the angel is bleeding again!" said Von Hulking, suddenly distracted.

Father Fritter sighed. "Twenty, but you're killing me here."

•••

Johnny Gestured To The opening of the cave. "It's kind of dank and slimy in there, but they seem to like it."

"All right, I can take it from here," said Van Hulking, shouldering the Master Blaster.

"Be careful, man," said Johnny. "These aren't like ordinary vampires. They're Vampussy. A whole different breed. They'll take your eyeballs out and use them for marbles."

"I've done my homework," said Von Hulking. "I can handle myself." He closed the visor on the helmet and tapped at the glass with one gloved finger. "Let them try to pierce this special extra-heavy glass, 19 mm of protection. They'll be in for a world of pain."

"What?"

"Sorry, forgot to turn on my head mike." Von Hulking pressed a button and the outside speaker crackled to life. "I said, this is more than two feet of extra-heavy glass. Like wearing a thick glass rubber, but on your head."

"Remember—they suck anything and everything. Blood, jizz, lymph, snot, it's all the same. You can't just stroll in there with bravado and a heart full of vengeance. You won't last three seconds."

"What about you? I thought were in this together, man!"

"I found their hideout, and I'll lay down a suppressing cover fire with the holy water, but I'm not going in there with you."

Von Hulking disappeared into the cave mouth. Five minutes later, the sound of screams, the flapping of leather wings, groans of agony and defiance and then an odd silence—followed by slushy submission--told Johnny everything he needed to know about their plan's outcome.

With a leaden heart, he dropped the Master Blaster squirt rifle on the ground and drove back to the city, chalking it all up to fate, kismet, karma and inevitability.

●●●

"Zo, Zat Ees Tha Story of how I became a rehab kounzeller. Hart there any qvestions?"

The room was silent except for the occasional chair squeak.

"Yes, ees that your hand up I see?"

"Well," said Lydia, "I think we've all learned a valuable lesson here. Don't you think?" She looked around the room. Her brothers and sisters in recovery nodded, many of them sheathed in bandages and missing limbs, eyes and ears. "It's said that an encounter with the shadow self means sacrifice of one kind or another, and those of us who don't have physical wounds have sacrificed in other ways. We all bear scars on the inside."

There was fervent agreement on this point.

"I think…" and her eyes began to well up. "I'm sorry, this is such an emotional subject for me. But I think we all deserve congratulations for making it this far. The road to recovery is long and painful, but, speaking just for myself, I feel optimistic. I think I'm going to make it. I think we're all going to make it. And thanks to our wonderful leader, Dr. Nico Puzbat, we can see what comes after. It won't be soft roses and plushy bears, but neither will it be night after night of blood orgies, dismemberment and self-mutilation. Am I right?"

"Zank you, Lydia," said Dr. Puzbat. "Defhinitally not plooshy bearz."

"But what about relapses?" asked Von Hulking, who wore a full body cast.

"Eez ok to tek a leetle neep now and again," said Dr. Puzbat. "Vee are only human. Vell, I personally am not, ha ha. But you know vat I mean."

Von looked deeply in Lydia's eyes, and then down at her shoulder, where a fresh bite mark oozed. Lydia shyly dropped her eyes. The two held hands.

"Defhinitially not plooshy bearz!" repeated Dr. Puzbat to relieved laughter and applause.

END.

–3– LOOKER

In my eyes
There's no one more lovely in all of the world
And she looks at me at times with such surprise
When she sees how special she is in my eyes.
--John Conlee, "In My Eyes"

AS FAR BACK AS SHE could remember, Eilish Kiernan had turned heads.

When she walked down the street, eyes followed her. A lot of eyes—old guys in garages who looked like they'd given up ever having a date with a real woman, slouched down in overalls, absently caressing a tailpipe like it was their cock; young strutters in board shorts, ripped, bulked out and knowing it—even girls, from the prim and proper to the slutty-looking, checked her out and liked what they saw.

She wondered just what that was, exactly. The Eilish that greeted her in the bathroom mirror each morning was nothing special, just plain old Ms. Kiernan, cute but not cover-model gorgeous, 5' 7," green eyes, ripples of red hair that curled down to her ass, Scots-Irish genes giving her skin the look of transparent milk, the blue lines in her eyelids visible, a patch of freckles symmetrically distributed across her face; a slightly protuberant bump on her nose, small ears and a cupids-bow mouth, small but well-formed breasts. As far as she was concerned, acceptable, pleasant, but hardly worth the attention.

Once an older dude had called her a "Looker," which when she thought about it was a funny word. Because she wasn't the one doing the looking. The word compressed someone else's desire into the desired object.

The eyes made her feel uneasy. Knots formed in the pit of her stomach. A hot flush crawled across her face. She felt like something in an aquarium, not quite human, not quite normal…not quite real.

The others saw things that weren't there. Not her soul, her brain, her intellect, just a rippling pattern of electrons bounced off her body and reformed in alien retina, a mirage, a ghost. Would they look at her the same way if she

were laid out on a mortician's prep table? Eilish
wondered.

She'd seen a movie once in which a
mortician fucks a fresh stiff. She knew, just knew,
that somewhere out there, somebody was
whacking off to that movie. Necrophilia, the
ultimate in objectification. Would her body be
fuckable, or wank-worthy, laid out like a Blue
Plate Special? Not that she cared, I mean, what
would she care, anyway, if she were dead?

The movie—by a Spanish director, Nachos
Bel Grande, something like that—flashed through
her mind whenever she was out in public,
shopping, sight-seeing, at a museum, out there in
the world she tried so hard to resist.

But she had to get out there, see and be
seen. It was necessary for her recovery, the doctor
had told her. She couldn't just sit in her
apartment and watch TV. There was a danger, the
doctor had said, of something called "de-
realization"—which meant losing touch with the
concrete, the tangible human reality.

Intellectually, she knew he was right, but
still, whenever someone looked at her that way,

she thought about the film. The lust in the doctor's eyes as he snapped photo after photo of the corpse, the fresh meat splayed out on the prep table, seizing it, documenting it, slavering for the deadness of it, the object. The Looker.

●●●

Two Years Ago, Eilish had been working at the post office. She was proud of her performance, glad to be doing something productive with herself, keeping a stable job, a government job.

Until the Incident, her "break" as the doctor called it. The day the foreman got too close.

●●●

I Don't Need This, thought Dr. Pansky as he flipped quickly through the chart. Maybe it's time to retire.

Dr. Lou Pansky—known simply as "Dr. Lou" to his millions of adoring fans—was a household name, an icon. He'd written a bestselling book on celebrity narcissism, hours and hours of therapy sessions with addled rock stars boiled down into nuggets of pure clinical insight, which were then dumbed down for the masses and further reduced to handy dictums that the man on the street might use to make his own ass-backward diagnoses. He made more money from his TV show than he made from his radio show, had just bought a second house, a yacht and an aquarium stocked with exotic fish. His stock had risen so high in his own mind, it seemed positively degrading to still see patients—at least patients who didn't make the Billboard charts and the cover of *Rolling Stone* on a regular basis.

Possible adult-onset schizophrenia, he noted. The patient was a 30-year-old woman in otherwise excellent health who had cut a deal with the court on an assault charge. What she had done to her supervisor at the post office turned even his stomach, and he'd seen a lot, like the smeared brains of a cop who'd made good on his threats to, as he called it, "terminate himself"—all over a parking space at Los De

Abajo Hospital. Dr. Lou's parking space, to be specific.

With this patient, Dr. Lou saw another self-termination just waiting to happen.

"So," said Dr. Lou, "why do you think you're here?"

The woman was easy on the eyes, he had to admit, a fine babe. Not in his professional opinion, of course, but in a non-clinical setting he could easily imagine her ass poured over his bed, cinched into a black corset, trembling as he filled her with his full eight inches of sausage meat. Green eyes, red hair, that wonderful, transparent skin Irish girls had, where you could see their veins. Obviously she didn't regard him with the same level of appreciation. She wouldn't even look at him.

Eilish, that was her name, Eilish Kiernan. A beautiful name for a beautiful lady who had admitted herself, her body at least, the remainder opaque even to practiced eyes. "Patient is in severe denial," read Dr. Zimmer's nearly-illegible scrawl on the admission notes, which had been simply taped into the folder, the transcription department having been shut down after a strange incident involving the hospital's Director of Communications, a street person and an online plea for a forced blow job.

And speaking of forced blow jobs, Dr. Lou wondered how those cupid's bow lips would feel on his cock, servicing him. But enough. She was, after all, a human being, and he was an acclaimed doctor. A healer, in fact, who had taken the hypocritical oath. Hippocratic, even.

Dr. Lou looked up from the chart, cleared his throat and adjusted his trendy, rimless glasses. This nut would be tough to crack. He hoped he had the chops to crack it before the nut's insurance ran out, and he had to use another parking space while guys in HazMat suits picked up the "medical waste," the skull fragments and brain chunks that had once belonged to a real person.

Eilish was dressed in a long denim skirt, a sweater with a black diamond pattern, no makeup, her hair severely constricted in a bun. She was hugging herself and rocking back and forth. Dr. Lou wondered if she might have autism as well. Was a person *with* autism, he corrected himself. These days you couldn't be too politically correct, especially with all the mad liberation groups that were cropping up like mushrooms in shit.

"Should I repeat the question?" he asked.

"I heard you the first time," said the woman, looking down at her hands. At least she had stopped the rocking motion. "I'm here because I lost it."

"Lost what?" asked Dr. Lou.

"The plot, the thing, you know—my mind."

Dr. Lou checked the chart again. "Apparently you attacked your supervisor at the post office. Did you know he had to have reconstructive surgery?"

"He did?" she asked, completely blasé. Of course she knew that, she'd made nationwide headlines, even set off a string off copycat assaults which had led the talking heads to opine about "our desensitized society" and "a nation of voyeurs." Total bullshit, of course, but it sold soap. A lot of soap.

"You nearly took out his eye. You're lucky he didn't press charges."

Because he knew I'd come back to finish the job, thought Eilish. That wasn't Christian forgiveness, it was just plain fear.

Dr. Lou nodded appreciatively, as though she'd said something. He took off his glasses and tapped them against the chart. His eyes were the palest blue, slightly bloodshot. Use Visine much? she mentally queried. Maybe he stayed up late counting paper, plunging his fingers through the cash like Scrooge McDuck in that old Disney comicbook. Come to think of it, Dr. Lou looked a lot like that webfooted multi-millionaire. Eilish smirked, a subliminal flash at the corner of her lips.

"What happened to, to set you off? Do you remember anything he might have done or said that could have been a trigger?"

"A trigger," she repeated, thinking of the fat barrel of a .45 pointed in Dr. Lou's eye, her finger squeezing off a shot. Homicidal ideation, suicidal ideation, possible homosexual exposure.

Psychotic break not otherwise indicated. Danger to self and others.

"Well, he was leaning on me. I'd just finished my route and was sorting through some stuff when he burst into my cube with his big fat hairy face, started yelling at me that I needed to sort through the circulars—you know, the ads that go with junk mail. Like it was critical I did that now. I was thinking, where's the fire?"

"When your supervisor approached you that way, how did it make you feel?"

"Mad. Angry. Frustrated. Uh, what do you think?"

"That's understandable," said Dr. Lou. "Anybody would be. Did you consider expressing your frustration, as you put it, with him?"

Eilish looked up, squarely meeting the shrink's eyes. "Sure," she said with a smirk. "That would go over well. The guy was a total asshole. Nobody could stand to work with him, they just endured him. Shut up and put up. He knew he was asking for something that wasn't necessary, I mean they're circulars, for fuck's sake. Sorry for the language, I just, well, it made me mad. I work really, really hard. I've always been that way."

"So you thought he was taking you for granted," said Dr. Lou. "Well again, that's very understandable. But you didn't think to talk it out with him?"

"You *don't get it*, Doc," she said, her voice rising sharply, her face flushing. "This wasn't about the job, it wasn't about the inserts, and it was about him getting close to me. I guess I'm sorry I put him in the hospital, but the guy is a total pervert."

"You think he had sexual intentions towards you?"

"Gee whiz, what a startling insight!" said Eilish. "I guess that's why they pay you the big bucks, Doc. Yeah, I think he wanted to get in my pants. I was the only woman in the department, and he took complete advantage. It was a very macho environment. I thought about filing sexual harassment charges, but that would just backfire. I mean, that place was the very definition of Old Boy's Club."

"Do you remember what happened then? After he approached you, I mean."

"No, I don't," she said. "I just remember his eyes. The way he was looking at me. Like an object, a thing." She shuddered and looked away.

"Did he make you feel objectified?" asked Dr. Lou.

Eilish remained quiet.

A minute ticked by. Then another.
Dr. Lou made a few cursory notes in the chart.

"I feel like we're making progress," he said after ten agonizing minutes of silence. "So why don't we make an appointment for next week? Meanwhile I'm going to put you in group therapy. It might be easier to talk to the other patients. I realize that this is bringing up a lot of emotions that you haven't processed yet, and the best thing is to get them out there so you can look at them, as it were. See the feelings for what they really are."

She nodded, but she wasn't listening. Not to Dr. Lou. He had the same look in his eyes that her supervisor had, just before the darkness

swam through her brain—like his eyes were
cocks, full of jelly.

But Eilish had made progress, a lot of
progress. She still didn't feel well enough to work
and get off disability, but she had eventually
stabilized under Dr. Lou's care. At least he'd
signed off on her. Not, she suspected, because she
was completely cured, but because some pencil-
pusher at the insurance company had noted the
costs of her care and checked off a box. That was
how it really worked.

•••

These Days, At Least Most days, she felt perfectly
normal, just a girl who liked to lounge around
her small, two-bedroom apartment drinking
chocolate milk from a Snoopy glass, listening to
Coltrane or Bach or Nina Simone or Peter Gabriel,
even some esoteric noise stuff from Japan. She
had a lot of interests that people called eccentric,
which was a polite way of saying they thought
she was crazy. Harmless crazy, of course, cute
crazy, crazy in that vulnerable, damaged–but–hot

way that instantly attracted men. What they didn't know, she thought, wouldn't hurt them.

And then there were the not-so-good days, when even little things bothered her, the neighbor's kids running around, dogs barking, helicopters, flies. Then she felt paper-thin, a permeable membrane; sounds seemed solid, the walls warped inwards, and she sat alone and held herself until the feeling passed.

On those days she felt like the original Lonely Girl. Nobody understood her. Nobody cared. And the worst thing of all—the gods' cruel joke on a woman everybody, apparently, wanted—was that Eilish couldn't release. Achieve the pleasure everybody else took for granted, an orgasm. Not even with herself.

Not that she hadn't tried. Jesus, she tried. She started going to bars, just sitting there nursing a gin and tonic, trying to loosen up. She got hit on almost instantly, and she forced herself to go through the motions, feeling like an alien just learning the ways of this particular planet.

These encounters were invariably disappointing. More often than not the guy couldn't get it up—small wonder after a night of drinking, quaffing down the social lubricant, staggering arm in arm back to his place or hers, it didn't really matter, hands fumbling at her skirt, stripping her down to her naughty underwear— she was meticulous in this, as with most things— which was wasted on the wasted.

Oh well, it's more common than you think, no, I don't think we should see each other again, and um, you can't stay the night. Sorry it didn't work out. And, well, see you around. Ritual sentences and phrases, formal modes of interaction that allowed everybody to save face and maybe live to fuck another day.

And even when it did work out, at least functionally, he got his rocks off and she was frustrated. Very frustrated. She would lay there and contemplate the cottage cheese pattern the plaster made on the ceiling and wonder if there was anything good on TV that she was missing because she was trying to get laid, get off, cum already. The man went up and down like a robot and she gave him what he wanted to hear, the whimpers, the sighs, the cries, as he did his best porno dude impression—*Oh, you like that honey? You like my big cock in your ass? Do you want to suck my hard cock?*—with thudding literalism, up and down, maybe a little sideways action, a little kink—*would you like me to tie you up? How about it baby? You like it rough?*

The answers to these and other frequently-asked questions boiled down to one: Yes and No. Yes, ideally I would respond well to your pathetic attempts at seduction you learned from watching skin flicks wanking off in your solitary bachelor bedrooms, but no, I don't find that a turn-on at all, but yes, I would probably find you a more-than-satisfactory lay if my pussy wasn't a polar vortex.

She'd tried everything, seeing a therapist—a woman who actually came on to her in the therapy session, not exactly professional; a sex surrogate (a really good-looking hunk of a guy with an enormous cock; she didn't come); a dominatrix who tied her to an X-cross, gagged her and spanked her ass with a crop whip (she almost came, but not because of the pain/pleasure factor, just because it was slightly different than the normal scene) but so far, nothing moved her. Nothing satisfied her.

Eilish Kiernan: Portrait of a Frigid Bitch.

Deep down, she knew exactly what was wrong. It was the eyes.

Their eyes locked her in. Like an iron corset. Like a thing in a box. She seemed to shrink to the size they could appreciate. And it wasn't a matter of insight, or intelligence, or sensitivity, or gender, sexual orientation—all eyes gave her the creeps, no matter who they belonged to.

Of course she could always blindfold them, which solved the problem, but that was almost worse, because then they had her image trapped in their brains and they were working it over behind the band of cloth.

One night Eilish was lying in bed as per usual, trying to get some of that good stuff people called Sleep, when a solution presented itself. Dr. Lou had mentioned something in one of their interminable sessions, something she hadn't especially impressed her at the time. He called it "aversion therapy," although her brain had translated the words into "a virgin therapy." Of course she didn't share the thought with him. She could just imagine the "aha" look in his eye, him asking her about her father, did he ever touch you, did he ever do anything that made you uncomfortable, perhaps your condition is related somehow to early childhood trauma, repressed memories, I can help you with that.

Sure he would help. That kind of help she didn't need. And after all, she wasn't a virgin, not by a long shot. She didn't have Daddy issues either, not even repressed ones. But something had clicked in her brain like one marble smacking up against another. And just as suddenly she was asleep.

The next morning she got up extra-early and, even before making coffee or taking a pee, Rita punched the on button and waited impatiently for her Mac to load. Then, she Googled "artificial eyes." There were over four million results.

The plan she'd formulated in a rush the previous night was still straightening itself out into an orderly progression of cause-and-effect steps; all she knew was that keying in her Visa card and hitting "send" made her kittie tingle.

●●●

Three Days Later, the eyes arrived at her doorstep. She tore open the package, lancing the cardboard with a pair of scissors, gouging several large holes in it, enough to get hand purchase, ripping it open and finally—her hand closed on another box, which was stuffed with Styrofoam peanuts, under which lay—the stuff wet dreams are made of.

Trembling with excitement, she placed the glass eyes on her comforter, then took one of the eyes in her hands.

It felt cold to the touch. She touched it, smelled it, even licked it. No papillary contraction, nothing remotely human—just a rather pleasing pattern of blue and white and black. This was one eye that could never capture her image, size her down to a fraction of herself, adjust her.

According to Dr. Lou, aversion therapy was a means by which how people overcame phobias by directly experiencing the things they feared most, in a safe environment of course. Almost giggling with glee, she placed the eyes in a row on her bookcase, wedging them in with globs of clay so they wouldn't roll off, lay back on the bed, spread her legs and began to touch herself.

They can't see me, Eilish reminded herself. They're dead. Better than dead—they were never alive to begin with. No optic nerve, so no problem. Electrons hit the glass and bounce back, that was it; no brain to connect with and send little synaptic fingers through an album of preset images with which the brain compared and contrasted the living, breathing organism beneath it with others, real and unreal, it found acceptable, arousing, worthy of a hard-on.

Slowly she moved her hand down past the damp red patch of pubic hair, to her clit, her aching clit...she slowly circled her forefinger around the clit while her other hand played with her pussy lips...there was no hurry, there was no time, no judgment to formulate…she stroked faster and faster as her other hand squeezed open her pussy walls, one finger, three fingers, wet and hot and slippery and in and out and out and in as the blank glass eyes looked down at her without seeing…she bit her lower lip and drew blood that trickled down her cheek and she deliberately licked it and found it good, salty, iron-rich, as her toes curled and her back arched and the warmth began in her feet and soared up her thighs and exploded in her pussy, sending tsunami waves of pleasure through her entire body…and again, and again, until she thought she was going to pass out it felt so fucking good.

As the clock kicked steadily and the eyes stood still.

She must have passed out for real then, because when the phone woke her up she automatically checked the time and it was a good four hours later.

"Hello?" she said.

"Hey, it's me—Frank. Frank Hill."

"Who?"

"Oh, you know, Frank. The guy with the goggles. We met at the High Life."

"Frank Hill with the goggles?" she nearly choked on her own laugh. "Sure, I remember you now."

And who could forget, Frank Hill with the goggles, something he'd read about in a book on how to pull females. Wear something unique and they'll remember you. Eilish had read the same book, of course—it was good to know the enemy's strategy.

"Anyway, I was just calling to see if you wanted to have lunch sometime, or dinner, or a movie, or just hang out..." He was starting to ramble on in a nervous Woody Allen way, snatch-grabbing goggles or no. What a geek.

"Are you doing anything right now?" she asked.

"Um, no. Are you?"

"Honey, I don't talk just to exercise my jaws. Why don't you come on over? Do you remember my street address?"

She hung up on Frank midway through a stuttered explanation about how he was going to go online and find a shortcut and he'd probably take his bike...details, details. It was as good an opportunity as any to check her self-constructed aversion therapy in a live setting.

●●●

Frank Hill Was Average in every conceivable way: average height, average build, average intelligence, average job, average cock size. He was one of nature's unfortunates in almost every respect. But he did have one feature that, to Eilish anyway, made him sexier than a Mr. Universe with a PhD in Astrophysics.

Frank Hill was blind in one eye.

Humming along to the classical radio station—she could barely concentrate on keeping the tune, not that it mattered whether it was Bach or Mozart or Beethoven or Mach of "Suck My Love Pump" fame—Eilish adorned herself. She put on her sexiest black lace bra, matching panties, black elbow-length leather gloves, garter belt and fishnet stockings.

The little black dress, a quick makeup job, and she was ready.

"The door's open," she said when she heard Frank Hill-the–guy-with goggles' timid knock. When he saw her lying on the bed, barely bothering to keep her skirt down, he looked stunned. Shocked. Like a little boy caught whacking it in the school lavatory.

"Hi," he said. "Um, what's up?"

"It's okay," said Eilish. "You don't have to make conversation. There's a bottle of wine in the fridge—pour yourself a glass if you like. Just relax, make yourself comfortable. *Mi casa es su casa.* Okay?"

"S-sure," he said, jolting for the kitchen and spilling half the wine on the sink. "I have a little drinking problem," he said, trying to save face. "Is this Cabernet Sauvignon?"

"It's the vino," she said. "Drink up."

He came near her and sat down in a chair in front of the bed.

"What are you doing so far away?" asked Eilish "Come on, big boy. It's your lucky day. A chance like this comes, oh, maybe once in a lifetime for a guy like you. I don't want to talk, I don't want to share my feelings, I just want you to fuck my brains out. Got it?"

Frank got up awkwardly from the chair and sat down on the bed.

"Not like that," said Eilish. "Do I have to do everything? Come on, relax." She closed her arms around him from behind and reached down and started stroking his cock. "There, isn't that better?"

Frank moaned as Eilish turned around to face him, pushed him down on the bed and began to vigorously suck him off. She licked his shaft up and down, deep-throated him and bobbed her head as he tried to play with her hair, splayed his fingers like a spastic, grunted, salivated and within five minutes splatter her Cupid's bow lips.

It tasted horrible, like a combo of wet dog, beer and stale coffee. She licked her lips and smiled. "Yummy," she said. "I want to taste every drop."

"Is there anything I can...do for you?" he asked. His cock was still hard.

In the way of response, she put her hand around his neck and gently–but–firmly pushed it down. After a few seconds of this he got the point, greedily, gratefully eating her pussy.

Eilish closed her eyes. It felt so good, she had almost forgotten the basic problem she was using Frank to analyze and correct.

She looked down. Frank was making happy gurgling sounds as he made up with enthusiasm what he lacked in job training. His left eye, the good one, was fixed up at her as though asking whether he was doing it right; his right eye, being made of glass, stayed in the same position.

Then her mood began to phase–shift. Deep inside, she knew something bad was about to happen. If she tried to analyze what exactly was going on, she'd kill the good feeling, waste a good lay, another chance at actual climax with a real live person.

But if she didn't figure it out…someone was going to get hurt.

The thought forced itself past the barrier she had tried to erect. The thought was, I hate the way he's looking at me.

He might as well be blind in both eyes, for all he can see me truly.

I'm a good person. An interesting person. I have a brain, a sense of humor, a personality. I'm not just the sum of my tits and ass. I listen to John Coltrane and Bach and Japanese noise. I like to lounge around in my pj's and drink hot chocolate. But he sees this…this thing…this shapely behind, this glistening pussy, as he dunks his head down like a dog slurping at his water dish, looking up at me for approval. He doesn't see me, not even with his one good eye.

And the blackness swarmed her brain. *And she saw herself reach down and clamp her fingers around the good eye and push and pull as her nails dug into the tender membrane and then it had exploded in her hand, some kind of clear gel that looked and felt exactly like lube, and she rubbed the gel against her pussy lips and it felt good, so achingly fucking good, and she dug in and got the whole eye, what was left of it, and stuck it inside her, jamming the optic nerve into her pussy so the eyeball was just sticking out of her labia, like something from a Surrealist painting, and through the black swarm she heard someone screaming, Frank Hill with the goggles was screaming and saying whatthafuck over and over, whatthafuck you cunt, you whore...her pussy walls squeezed around the thick nerve, better than any cock in the world, and she was lost in her own universe, a thick, viscous atmosphere, like opium...she was having the weirdest thoughts too, like her pussy could see through Frank's eye—now in new, improved PUSSYVISION—the walls warping around her but it was safe now, she was safe to breathe, safe to see, safe to cum...she saw lightning flash behind her eyes as her climax shuddered through her, legs trembling, coating her thighs with kittiejuice, coming ten times as hard as she had by herself with just the glass eyes planted like disembodied voyeurs on her bookcase...*

When Eilish's head had cleared she saw Frank lying in the fetal position, his left eye still oozing blood, mucus and gel, drooling and muttering to himself like an idiot. "Shhhh," she said, placing a hand on his shoulder. He flinched slightly but said nothing coherent.

"You're in luck," Eilish said. "I just happen to have some extra glass eyes, oh, lying around. All we need to do is clean out that socket and let the wound heal. That'll take, what, maybe a week, two weeks?"

Frank nodded and moaned. She noticed, but without emotion, that he'd soiled himself. That she could take care of too.

Eilish felt so much better about everything.

Looking down, she realized that the eyeball was still sitting in her pussy. That was okay, she thought. At least it couldn't watch her anymore.

Now, for the first time, she really did feel like a Looker.

END.

–4– DEATH CAT AND STORM CROW ARE FRIENDS

1. Death Cat and Storm Crow Might Be More Than Friends …

AT FIRST, DEATH CAT AND STORM CROW were not friends. Or rather, they had the potential to be friends, but only after bridging some misunderstandings between them.

Death Cat found Storm Crow annoying because every time he walked down to the cantina to have a beer and compose his long, mournful love songs, Storm Crow would be perched on a fence or in a tree or on a railing, teasing him.

Storm Crow was secretly in love with Death Cat but hid her true feelings behind taunts and jests. She thought it was cute the way he strutted along in his self-constructed uniform with gold braids and epaulettes, seemingly without a care in the world, yowling improvised lyrics directed at Melissa or Candy or Sarah or whoever tickled his fancy at the time. The truth is that Storm Crow was jealous but not aware that she was. So she called: "Hey Death Cat, who is she this week?"

Death Cat either ignored the crow or hissed at her. Storm Crow fluttered her blue-black wings in mock fear, but stayed put on the fence or tree or railing, and teased him some more.

"Love the costume, Death Cat! Who are you supposed to be, Sergeant Pepper? Andy Gibb?"

Occasionally Death Cat lost his composure and chased Storm Crow, who soared in circles, calling "too slow!"

"One of these days," Death Cat muttered. "If I only had a good slingshot. Or an air rifle."

"Like to see you try!" cawed Storm Crow.

One day Death Cat passed out in front of the cantina. Storm Crow walked right up to him and flapped her wings in his face. Then she retrieved a mirror from a pouch she carried around her neck and held it up to his mouth.

When he awoke, he was startled to see his avian nemesis.

"We have mist," said Storm Crow.

"Listen, Storm Crow," said Death Cat. "I don't feel like fighting today. Would you like to hang out, maybe take in a movie, have a cup of coffee?"

Storm Crow's heart skipped a beat. "Really?" she squawked. "I'd love to. Say, who's buyin'"?

"The java's on me," said Death Cat. He picked up his guitar and strummed a few sour chords. "Need to tune this up."

"Say," said Storm Crow. "I always meant to ask you. How come you're always singing about girls? Are these real cats or imaginary ones?"

Death Cat looked distressed. For a second he froze and Storm Crow could see right through him, straight to the bones. She was shocked. Death Cat's eyes disappeared and tiny tombstones spun in his sockets. Storm Crow shrieked and fell over in a dead faint.

When she awoke, Death Cat was tenderly holding her and caressing her wings. "I'm sorry," he said. "Didn't mean to scare you. But your question—it goes deep. I once had a love; her name was Emily. She was a parrot, actually. One look at her green plumage and I was a goner. I used to just hang out and watch her. Finally, I summoned up the courage to say something. I told her how I felt. How, even though I'm a cat, and a Death Cat at that, I love…birds. And not just how they taste. Well, Emily caught part of it and I thought she said she loved me. Oh, I was in heaven. All my songs were about her—Emily the Parrot. Until one day, I was going to surprise her, and I snuck up behind her when she suddenly started repeating 'I love birds, I love birds.' I knew right then and there that it was over. The love between two species…it never works."

Storm Crow looked sad. Then she had a hopeful thought. "Maybe she was just repeating what you said. Isn't that what parrots do?"

"You mean…"

"I mean I know birds. Heck, I am one. But there's birds and birds. Parrots aren't the smartest in the flock. Yeah, they look pretty, but they're dumbbells. Not an original thought in the whole bunch."

"Hmmm…" Death Cat thoughtfully scratched his nose with a paw. "I guess I was too busy feeling bad to consider that. So who are the smart birds?"

"Honey, you're looking at the smartest."

No longer transparent, Death Cat popped back his eyes to replace the tombstones. "Say something smart."

Afterwards, as they lay in a sticky pile, Storm Crow gently brushed the cat's brow with her feathers. "Tell me something, lover," she said.

Death Cat purred contentedly. "Sure. What would you like to know?"

"Well, I always wondered about your name. I've seen the tombstones now and when you get anxious your fur and skin goes all transparent. But what's the real story? How did you get to be Death Cat?"

"Okay. Well, one day I was just sitting on the back porch, playing some old bluegrass music, when I felt this chill go right through me.

Like someone stepped on my shadow's tail, you know?"

"Uh-huh."

"And there was this voice: 'You will be Death Cat. Yours is the power to summon the dead from their graves, for one night only.'" Suddenly I could see right through myself. I looked in a mirror and there were these tombstones sitting there where my eyeballs used to be. I found out that if I breathed slowly through my nose and out my mouth, I could reset myself. But yeah, if I get startled—pop, out go the eyes, in come the tombs.

I'm used to it by now. Only I've never actually summoned the dead. Waiting for the right night, I guess. How about you? What's the word on Storm Crow?"

"I can control weather with my beak," said Storm Crow.

"Wow."

"It's no big thing."

They cuddled some more.

*2. Death Cat and Storm Crow Might Have Been
Friends …*

Had They Ever Met. But Death Cat was always busy with his guitar practice, and Storm Crow became deathly ill one day when a tsunami and a hurricane caught in her throat. Death Cat stopped going to the cantina because he wanted to get serious about music. He began to read *Guitar Player* and studied scales night and day, even very exotic scales like the mixolydian. His paws raced up and down the fretboard and soon he was blazing out riffs that combined the peasant songs of ancient Greece with progressive black metal, reminiscent of his now-favorite band, Rotting Christ. When Storm Crow emerged from her convalescence, Death Cat was headlining Germany's Wacken Festival and set that year's record for blowing speakers.

Storm Crow saw a YouTube video of Death Cat's performance and felt the immediate thrill of recognition. "We might have been friends," she croaked plaintively, tucking her head beneath her wings. "Or even more—but that is life." Storm Crow vomited extreme weather until the planet reeled.

3. Death Cat and Storm Crow Are at Odds ...

One Day Storm Crow was sitting on a fence post thinking of ways to alter the weather when Death Cat reeled out of the cantina, dead drunk, walked into a tree, hit his head and knocked himself out.

As soon as consciousness left him, the tombstones buried deep within his eyes took flight, whirring through the air as they flashed arbitrary inscriptions. Storm Crow saw them coming but not in time to duck, and the left eye tombstone pushed her from her perch.

As it happened, right beneath the fence post lay a pool of mud subtly tainted with toxic waste, and Storm Crow fell right in. Her soiled wings took on a green glow and the weather she directed with her beak boiled with poisonous chemicals.

Storm Crow was quarantined by the Center for Disease Control, which gave her time to think. She recalled the tiny letters chipped in the tombstone's granite, spelling out terrible omens meant only for her. At the very bottom of the tombstone the words "Just Kidding" and a whiskered emoticon appeared. Frustrated and piqued, Storm Crow began to conceive plans to avenge herself against Death Cat.

When Death Cat woke up, he felt better than ever. The sophisticated scales he had practiced finally felt like a part of him. Picking up his guitar, he began to play, faster and faster, until all of nature fell into sympathetic accord. He yowled, squealed, cried, moaned and hit the fretboards hard, which produced artificial harmonics echoed in the slant of the sun on buildings and the way air caressed certain early morning joggers. The longer Storm Crow was quarantined, people and critters who associated weather control with the bird shifted their allegiance to the cat.

When Storm Crow was finally released, she walked straight into the cantina, where Death Cat was playing to a rapt audience, flew at his guitar and attacked it with her beak. After repeated assaults, the guitar neck hung limply askew from its body, the strings were undone, and Death Cat was howling with such anger that he made the clouds burst and the rivers rise. The cantina with all its customers was carried far out to sea.

Bobbing up and down in the waves, Death Cat used a piece of his demolished guitar as a life raft. Storm Crow skimmed above his head and squawked, "thanks for the tombstones, cat. And for stealing my thunder. You are such a bastard."

"Have it all back," said Death Cat. "I'm sorry for everything. Could you just please get me to dry land?"

Satisfied that she had made her point, Storm Crow opened her beak and let out a hurricane force wind. Death Cat sailed across the sea until he arrived above the cantina. Storm Crow appeared behind him as he dusted himself off and was about to enter the bar. "I don't think so," she squawked. "Unless you leave your tombstones at the door. They might injure somebody."

"Don't need the stones to drink," said Death Cat. "Hey, can I buy you a beer?"

"Thanks, but no," said Storm Crow. "I have a reputation to rebuild."

"Sorry, again."

"It happens," said Storm Crow, perching herself on top of the tombstones. "Go on, have a drink. I'll watch these for you."

4. Death Cat and Storm Crow: A Philosophical Disagreement ...

Always One For Self-Improvement, Storm Crow returned to school and began to study philosophy. She was most impressed with the Idealist concepts propagated by Immanuel Kant, which she applied to Hegel's dialectical structures with astonishing results. Eventually, she theorized, all beings would achieve a state of union with a supreme, transcendental reality.

Under the influence of Greek Black Metal, Death Cat had followed another direction in his own, self-directed course of study. He picked up on the theory of negative dialectics espoused by postmodern followers of Friedrich Nietzsche, and showed up uninvited at Storm Crow's seminars.

He amused himself by running across the tables and desks yowling "Hegel was a fraud" and "turn them dialectics upside down."

When a restraining order failed to alter Death Cat's behavior, Storm Crow went online and began to research alternatives. Scrolling through pages on EBay, she hit on the perfect solution: a cartoon shotgun, formerly owned by Elmer Fudd, which blasted pure dialectic bullets. Moreover, the gun was surprisingly cheap, despite being in near-new condition. After a successful bid, she practiced in her backyard, shooting at paper targets of Death Cat.

The next time Death Cat showed up at a seminar, Storm Crow was ready for him. He was a little unsteady on his paws, having by this time become an addict of Schrodinger's Catnip. He thumped the podium and was about to embark on a vicious attack on Hegel when Storm Crow flew down, holding the Fudd Gun in her claws.

"Just one second, Mister Death Cat," she squawked. "I want you to walk away from the podium, very slowly. Then make a beeline for the door before I open up with this here weapon."

When Death Cat ignored her and continued with his prepared speech, Storm Crow squeezed the trigger. The dialectical bullets took opposing trajectories and then fused into a synthetic superbullet that shattered Death Cat's right tombstone. Frantically clawing at his eye, Death Cat leapt down from the podium and slunk out the door.

5. After Exchanging Identities, Death Crow and Storm Cat Write Their Memoirs ...

Actually, This Never Happened.

6. Life Cat and Calm Crow are Friends ...

Many Years Later, Death Cat had a spiritual awakening and set aside his tombstone eyes, replacing them with twin suns. Around the same time, Storm Crow became tired of extreme weather and embarked on a journey of self-discovery. To this day they live a thoroughly tranquil, if somewhat boring, existence, contemplating the clouds and playing a non-combative game they call "Peace Chess."

7. *Schrodinger's Catnip ...*

On A Government Grant to isolate the psychoactive properties in catnip, Dr. Death Cat made a startling discovery. Using a cold water process, he dissolved the catnip into fine granules. After letting the powder dry overnight, he ingested about 10 grams. Within minutes, Dr. Death Cat found himself splitting into two quantum states. In one, he was alive and had gone back to playing his guitar at the cantina; in the other, he was dead and his tombstone eyes had developed into catacombs piled with the bones of his alternate selves.

"You've changed, man," said Storm Crow, who was going through a neo-Beatnik phase. "You're all split apart now, Daddy O."

"Go back to playing your bongos," said the live, guitar-playing version of Dr. Death Cat. The dead Dr. Death Cat pulled Storm Crow into his catacombs. Storm Crow revolted at the strewn

skeletons, fractal variants on the original Dr.
Death Cat. She opened her beak wide and a
thunderstorm broke, scoring and scattering the
bones with thick shafts of lightning. The water
level in the catacombs got higher and higher and
soon the bones began to flow from Dr. Death
Cat's sockets, along with Storm Crow.

Once the catnip formula had worn off,
Death Cat locked his notes on the experiment in a
fire safe, together with the cold water extract.

Meanwhile, Storm Crow had outgrown
her neo-Beatnik phase and was working for the
Man, whose name was Henry. Henry disapproved
of Storm Crow's friendship with Death Cat and,
sadly, Storm Crow's need for a job overrode her
affection for the feline guitarist cum quantum
puzzle. It was only much, much later when the
economy completely collapsed, Henry landing
somewhere soft in his golden parachute, Death
Cat mournfully strumming the chords to "I Loved
a She-Crow Making Weather with Her Beak,"
that Storm Crow walked into the ruins of Death
Cat's laboratory and made her apologies. "There's
no need," said Death Cat, whose eye sockets now

spurted St. Elmo's Fire. "You did what you had to do. *Sauve que peut*, as they say."

8. Stormdeathcrowcat Forever ...

Storm Crow Hadn't Seen her good friend Death Cat in a very long time. Curious, she flew on down to the cantina and waited. She saw Death Cat coming and was about to say hello when he ducked down an alley behind the cantina, his head down, deep in thought. Storm Crow followed at a discreet distance and saw him enter the partially burned laboratory in which he had experimented with the quantum catnip.

Death Cat took a ball of yarn from a green steel desk and began to play with it. Storm Crow hovered in the doorway and watched as Death Cat looped the yarn between his paws and stretched them apart. She saw that the yarn string was made of distinctly colored lengths, no two the same. Intrigued, she flew down onto the desk. So concentrated was Death Cat that he barely noticed his old pal.

"Watcha doing?" asked Storm Crow.

"I'm meditating," said Death Cat.

"With yarn? How do you meditate with yarn?"

"Look very carefully," said Death Cat. Storm Crow came closer. "No, through the magnifying glass." She picked up the magnifying glass and held it over the ball of yarn. "Oh my," she said.

"What do you see?"

"All our adventures, every variation and combination. All the things we've been through together—it's all there. When you pull at the ball, it changes the narrative mix. Wow. So here's you and me in Victorian England arguing about the aphrodisiac properties of carrots. And here we're lovers in a turn of the century bordello in New Orleans. In this one, we will never meet. In that one, we're about to merge our identities and put on a spectacular show at the cantina. A show to end all shows. I see feathers flying and fur spraying."

Death Cat put the ball down on the desk. "Let me sing you a song," he said. And he began to play guitar, faster and faster till the planet's rotation increased dramatically, and the two friends found themselves flying through the air in the company of trees, cows and a troupe of bewildered Boy Scouts. When he realized it was his guitar style that had caused these peculiar effects, he began to slow down. The trees rerooted themselves and the cows went back to pasture, but the Boy Scouts would never be quite the same.

"Okay," said Death Cat, somewhat chagrined. "I'll play you a different song. Something a little more mellow. Would you like to sing harmony?"

"My voice is kind of raucous," said Storm Crow.

"How about adding some cowbell, then?" said Death Cat.

Storm Crow began to bang the cowbell in time to the rhythm of Death Cat's new song, which was based on the yarn's prophecy that soon they would fuse together and become a formidable unit, a single beast with tombstone eyes that made weather, played guitar and cowbell and summoned the dead to life for one night only.

So the flyers went up and the word spread about a unique performance at the cantina. The town hadn't seen this kind of excitement since the last fusion of creatures a quarter-century before, an excitement that quickly turned to disappointment and a cry for refunds. Angrygopherat barely managed a few halting notes on the clarinet before they were booed off the stage. Nobody knew what had happened to them since, although one old timer claimed he had seen them spring from a laundry basket *with deadly intent.*

First, however, Death Cat and Storm Crow had to figure out a way to merge into a single being. Stormcatdeathcrow was just a dream at first, but after several failed attempts involving gum, bailing wire and seltzer water, they achieved oneness.

All the creatures came to the cantina to watch the performance. They filled up the tables and jammed themselves into corners and rattled the rafters. When Stormcatdeathcrow failed to appear, they hooted and hollered and stomped their feet and shook their claws and paws and hooves. After an interminable pause, the hybrid took the stage, strapped on the guitar and started to play.

The songs were a revelation. They seemed to cover the entire spectrum of emotion, even subtle, evanescent feelings such as the regret after the night's third beer summons a medley of Irish folk tunes from a childhood in Belfast. With the steady clack of the cowbell reinforcing the guitar's rhythm, Stormcatdeathcrow hissed and squawked through a program that took the audience from grandiose summits hurtling down to mundane valleys, with stops along the way that invoked the careening melodies of a steam calliope and the whimper of whipped pianos.

Slowly, gradually, the dead began to ooze from their graves. Drawn by the power of the music, they shambled to the cantina and choked the air with the smells of decayed flesh and grave cloth. The cantina's manager fussed about with a can of Lysol, but the odor sank into the wood and was present as an overly sweet, cloying smell for years to come.

After the set, Stormcatdeathcrow signed autographs, talked with fans and hawked an album, *Songs We Made as a Single Beast.* The show had been a huge success. There was just one problem: during the performance, the creature started to fall apart.

First the gum gave out, then the bailing wire, and finally the seltzer water. When the time came for an encore, Stormcatdeathcrow was held together only by willpower. As its yolked vocal chords screeched out the evening's last song, "Que Sera, Sera," a rumbling started in the claws and ran up through the furred feathers. The tombstones fell from the creature's eyes and landed with a squishy thud on a titmouse. Gasps of dismay and horror ran through the crowd. The head exploded, splashing the audience with a steaming mix of worm bile, sour milk, blood and phlegm. Then came the torso. The legs were the last to go, and strange legs they were, wrapped in a pelted plumage.

After a long and painful process of cellular reconstruction, the two friends decided to remain distinct.

9. Epilog …

"Well, We've Come To The End of the story," said Death Cat. "Do you think readers will be satisfied?"

"I don't know," said Storm Crow. "The narrative is unorthodox. It's more of a picaresque structure, a series of episodes, like *Don Quixote.*"

"And the problem with that is?"

"I got no problem with it," said Storm Crow. "Hey, have I ever told you how cute you look in that mariachi outfit?"

"Every day, baby," said Death Cat. "And I love it."

THE END-END

IN GARRETT COOK'S MURDERLAND serial killers are idolized by society. Their deeds are followed obsessively by television pundits and the adoring public. A subculture has grown up around this phenomena, called "Reap." Laws are created to allow this activity to flourish, including designated "safe zones' where killers can practice their trade without fear of persecution. Fans of the top rated serial killers celebrate each new kill on social media and television. Programs glorify their deeds.

The culture of Murderland is violent and mirrors our own violent society and its decadent obsessions; but Murderland isn't about how violent the world has become. It's about the pervasive nature of media and how it corrupts. It corrupts absolutely.

At the heart of Murderland is Jeremy Jenkins. Jeremy doesn't like what he sees and he's just enough insane to believe he can do something about it, that he can change the world. His methods are extreme- to outdo the serial killers, he'll kill THEM, turn their own twisted reality back on themselves. It's a hopeless task, impossible, Herculean; but it's Jeremy's fate to see it through to the end.

The three sections of Murderland comprise a true Homeric epic. In the first section we are shown the terrible world Jeremy lives in, the world that if we look at it honestly, is really our own world. We meet all the principal characters, the serial killers, the pundits, the pawns, and Jeremy's beloved Cass. In the second section Jeremy goes on a bit of a spiritual quest and comes to understand his true purpose. In the final section the flames are ignited and all hell breaks loose. Jeremy, like a great epic hero must journey to the underworld and be reborn in order to triumph.

BORN WHOLE FROM THE RECTUM of a dying patient, Morbid silently stalks the hospital's hallways, heinously dispatching the most helpless of patients and in the most painfully repulsive of manners. In the meantime, in order to pay for his family and home that includes his ghost step-father Sammy and his pet aborted fetus Chip, Westphal has to ingest mounds of dangerous narcotics to get through his night shifts. Barely hanging on to his Care Tech gig by his fingernails, the last thing Westphal needs is to be accused of Morbid's evil deeds. You, on the other hand, simply want to find some solace. Terminally ill from a virulent infection, and dependent on Life Support, all You beg for is a peaceful and dignified demise. Shirk has other plans for You. The ancient drug-snuffling demon makes You relive all of your deadly and venial sins as he tortures You. Night after night.

Until eternal Damnation begins for YOU MORBID WESTPHAL, yet again....

WICKED CANDY

Alex S. Johnson

IT LOOKS LIKE CAROLYN AND MARK are in deep, deep shit... Mark and Carolyn live in an alternate 1989 where Ronald Reagan is on his fourth presidential term. The USA has a rigid, long-standing caste system and abortions were never made legal. Being homeless is a crime that is

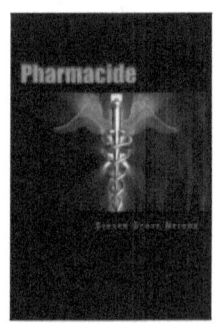

punishable by imprisonment in an internment camp the inmates call Tent City. Most of Mark's ER patients are inmates at this camp and are victims of a new disease these illegals call the Transient Flu. This deadly and rapidly spreading disease mutates with each new host, collecting information, changing code. The disease evolves lightning quick, spreading like pond ripples and infecting everyone. No one is safe. Mark and Carolyn dig too deep and uncover the brutal truth: Transient Flu was purposely made and is one hundred percent fatal. Carolyn's employer, Hudson-Smythe Pharmaceuticals, discovers the chain of evidence. It traces the pharmacide back to Hudson-Smythe and the crime of the century. Cost is no object and deadly force is authorized. Yes. Carolyn and Mark are in deep, deep shit.

IMMANUEL THE CHRIST HAS SOME NERVE. Jonah has already lost everyone he loves to Pilate the vampire and his Harbor drug violence. Jonah now trudges through his days staying as high on Plata as possible. He just wants to be left alone while he waits for his turn to die. The Christ has other plans for him. She sends Her messenger, Pedro, to assign Jonah the very dangerous task of ordering the Herod to dismantle the Harbor's Plata trade. Jonah decides to run.

But you can't run from God forever. As Jonah learns the hard way when the 'Edmund Fitzgerald' founders and goes down in rough seas, with the reluctant prophet on board.

Job is Satan's Chosen One and he doesn't take kindly to orders from some upstart prophet. Rather than acquiescing, Job thinks caving Jonah's head in with a tire iron is the best bet. Jonah finds himself out of the frying pan, but firmly fixed in the fire. Then the Lord Herself starts dispatching Job's children. One at a time, until the Herod of The Harbor finally obeys.

LINES TELL TALES THAT WITHOUT THE RIGHT EXPOSURE
live completely disguised within crevices that no amount of
washing can remove. Though we yearn to have them clean
– enough. Spend hundreds of dollars on this or that to wash
... them ... clean. But some stains never come out, no matter
how much we scrub, steam, or sterilize. And what becomes
of the hands that are soaked in generations of sins
committed by their owners, perpetual motion of offenses
against their fellow man time and time again? Isn't there
something that we've all done that we just can't seem to
cleanse ourselves from? And what if you were Pilate?
Steven Rage's "Pilate: A Brutal Bible Tale" explores the
depths of sin, the way it stains our lives, and graphically
illustrates the things we fear most.

"I'M FEELING DOWN AND DIRTY, feeling kind of mean, so I give those fans my middle finger. Those poor bastards go nuts. My team looks at me in awe. My coach frowns and the opposing one begins to furiously scratch out new plays. The Warface is feeling her oats tonight and they all know they're in for a deep snag. I see our opponents and I almost feel sorry for the poor bastards. Their fans can't help them. Their coach can't help them. I'm going to run them off their own track in front of their own fans and there is not one thing they can do about it. I see my counterpart positioning herself on the outside line. I've got my eye on her and I've got her number. She is going nowhere. I'm going to body check her narrow ass off the track and into the third row. I hear the second whistle sound. The jammers are starting to move behind us as I veer toward her. I lower my right shoulder. She sees me at the last second. I smile as her eyes open wide. I get speed, lean in deep and hit her. Silly rabbit, no one gets past the Warface. Not tonight they don't.

Another Road:

MYTH AND PAVEMENT IN THE AMERICAN IMAGINATION

By
Edward Caudill

Hidden **Mentor**

MEDIA

Hidden Mentor Media

Hardback: 979-8-9893121-7-7
Paperback: 979-8-9893121-6-0
Ebook: 979-8-9893121-8-4

Published by Hidden Mentor Media

Cover: Roadside culture by Jim Stovall, watercolor
it's a classic bit of Americana, replete with the roadside idlers, the all-purpose store, a crank-handle gas pump, and even a bench to complement the leisure time. We've all been there, whether then or in its modern incarnation. (Cover and watercolor by Jim Stovall)